Me and Neesie

by ELOISE GREENFIELD

illustrated by moneta barnett

Thomas Y. Crowell Company
New York

Other Books by Eloise Greenfield

ROSA PARKS

SISTER

PAUL ROBESON

Manufactured in the United States of America

Library of Congress Cataloging in Publication Data

Greenfield, Eloise. Me and Neesie. SUMMARY: Janell tells what happens to her invisible friend, Neesie, when Aunt Bea comes to visit. I. Barnett, Moneta, ill. II. Title. PZ7.G845Me [E] 74-23078 ISBN 0-690-00714-0 ISBN 0-690-00715-9 lib. bdg.

10   9   8   7   6   5   4   3   2   1

For my niece
Shelley Renee Black
and for all of her friends
that only she could see

It was a good thing for Neesie that Mama couldn't see her, or she would have got a good spanking.

Mama couldn't hear her either, but I could. All the time Mama was cornrowing my hair, Neesie kept calling me and waving her arms around, trying to make me look at her. After a while, I got tired of it.

"Stop it, Neesie!" I said. I couldn't play with her all the time, even if she was my best friend.

Mama pulled my head back around. "Keep your head still, Janell," she said. "And stop talking to yourself."

"I was talking to Neesie, Mama," I said.

"Nobody's in this bedroom but me and you," Mama said. "So if you not talking to me, you talking to yourself."

"Your mother don't know nothing," Neesie said. She made a face at Mama.

I got scared just thinking about Mama seeing her. Sometimes Mama plays games, but she don't never play games like that.

Mama finished my hair and patted it. I could tell I looked pretty by the way she was smiling at me.

She said, "Your father ought to be getting back from the train station with Aunt Bea in a little while. You want to help me fix her lunch?"

"Don't go, Janell," Neesie said. "Let's stay in here and play store."

I didn't know which one I wanted to do. I said, "Mama, Neesie wants me to play with her."

Mama held her forehead with her hand like she had a headache or something. Then she put her hand on my shoulder and bent down and looked right in my eyes.

"All right, Janell," she said. "But after Aunt Bea gets here, I don't want to hear another word about that Neesie mess. I guess I can stand you making up a friend, but Aunt Bea's old and nervous, and I don't want you upsetting her. You hear me?"

I said, "Neesie's not made up, Mama. She's real!"

"You hear me, Janell?" Mama said.

I told Mama all right, but I wasn't sure I could do it. It was hard not to talk about Neesie when she was always doing things. Right now, she was rolling on the floor and laughing, and I knew she was thinking about Aunt Bea being nervous.

I tried to keep from laughing, but I couldn't. I put my hand over my mouth and pointed at Neesie. I knew if Mama could see her squinching up her eyes and kicking her skinny legs, she would laugh, too. But Mama just shook her head and went out.

Neesie was laughing so hard, she rolled over on top of my new school shoes.

"Move, Neesie!" I said. "You messing up my school shoes!"

She sat up. I thought she was going to yell back at me like she always does, but she looked like she was going to cry.

I went and sat down beside her.

"What's the matter?" I asked.

"Nothing," she said.

I said, "We going to school tomorrow, remember?"

Neesie didn't say anything. She had her head down, and I leaned way over so I could see her face better. "Mama said school's going to be fun," I told her.

Then we heard Daddy's voice, and Neesie forgot she was sad. She jumped up and ran down the hall. I wanted to yell at her to come back, but I remembered what I had promised Mama. So I didn't say anything. I just ran down the hall behind her.

Aunt Bea was standing in front of the sofa, lean-
ing heavy on her walking stick and not letting
Daddy and Mama help her. Neesie jumped up on
the sofa and sat right behind her.

I said, "Hi, Aunt Bea." But I was looking at Neesie, and Mama was looking at me looking.

"Janell, baby!" Aunt Bea said. "You pretty as ever. Soon as I sit down, I want you to come over here and give me a great big hug."

Neesie was still sitting. She was grinning her bad grin, 'cause she knew I wouldn't let nobody mash her.

I opened my mouth to tell Aunt Bea to move over some, but Daddy reached for her arm.

"Aunt Bea," he said, "why don't you sit over here in this chair?"

"Keep your hands off me, Walter," Aunt Bea said. "Just keep your hands off me. I know where I want to sit and I don't need no help."

I saw her knees bend and her bottom start going down.

"Aunt Bea!" I yelled. "Don't sit on Neesie!"

Aunt Bea said, "Huh? Walter! Is that child seeing ghosts?"

Daddy said, "Take it easy, Aunt Bea, it's just . . ."

But Aunt Bea didn't take it easy. She said, "I'll get it!"

She held onto the arm of the sofa and swung her stick up in the air. She started beating up the sofa.

Neesie was yelling, "Help! Help!" and scooting around to get out of the way. She crawled down to the other end of the sofa, and then she just sat there looking silly like I did one time when I fell down in the store.

"Did I get it, Janell?" Aunt Bea asked. "Did I get it?"

I couldn't talk right then. And Mama couldn't
talk either. She was holding her forehead.
 But Daddy said, "I think you got it, Aunt Bea."

Neesie slid down off the sofa. "Let's go back in your room, Janell," she said.

I didn't answer her. I didn't want that stick to start flying again. I just said, "I'll be right back, Aunt Bea."

I closed my door so Aunt Bea wouldn't hear me talking. Neesie still had that silly look on her face, and I wanted to laugh, but I didn't want to make her feel bad.

"Aunt Bea's tough, ain't she?" Neesie said.

I said yeah Aunt Bea sure was tough.

Neesie said, "You can laugh if you want to, Janell. I don't care."

But I wasn't sure.

Then Neesie started laughing, and so did I.

"That's what I get, huh, Janell?" she said. "That's what I get for trying to be so smart."

We put our heads under the pillow so nobody could hear, and we laughed a long time.

But the next morning, Neesie was sad. She wouldn't get up. I wanted to go to school, but she didn't. She kept her head under the covers while Mama helped me get ready.

When me and Mama got outside, I heard Neesie
calling me, and I looked up at the window. She was
waving, and I waved back.

I didn't think about Neesie too much at school. I had a whole lot of fun with my new friends and my teacher. But when I got home, I wanted to tell Neesie all about it. Only, I couldn't find her. I looked all over and she wasn't there.

I called Mama.

"Shhh," Mama said. "Aunt Bea's trying to sleep."

"Mama," I said, "I can't find Neesie."

Mama said, "You can't?" She looked glad and sorry at the same time. She put her arm around me. "Want me to read you a story?" she said.

I said, "I don't care."

Mama sat in the big chair, and I sat on my little stool and leaned on her lap. She was reading to me, but I wasn't listening. I was thinking about how sad Neesie looked waving to me out the window. And about how she was my best friend and I didn't have nobody to play with before she came.

And then, I got tickled thinking about how silly she looked when she laughed and all the fun we had.

And then, I thought about going to school the next day and playing with my new friends. And I wouldn't never tell them about Neesie. 'Cause she was mine. Just mine.

And then, I put my head on Mama's lap like I always do and listened to her read.

About the Author

Eloise Greenfield is the author of several books for children and, since 1965, her short stories and articles have appeared in *Black World, Ebony Jr!, Scholastic Scope,* and other magazines.

Ms. Greenfield was born in Parmele, North Carolina. She grew up in Washington, D.C., where she now lives with her husband and family. She is the mother of a son, Steve, and a daughter, Monica. A former member of the D.C. Black Writers' Workshop, she has headed both the Adult Fiction and the Children's Literature Divisions. In 1973 she was Writer-in-Residence for the D.C. Commission on the Arts.

For her Crowell Biography *Rosa Parks,* published in 1973, Ms. Greenfield won the first Carter G. Woodson Award for Social Education. Whether writing biography or fiction, she says, "I want to give children words to love, to grow on."

About the Artist

Moneta Barnett lives and works in Brooklyn, where she was born. She studied art at the Brooklyn Museum Art School and at Cooper Union. For a time after graduation she worked in a design studio and then was art director in a serigraphics house. Now she happily concentrates on the illustrating of children's books.